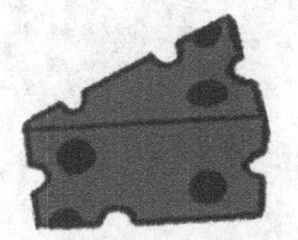

RATNiP
Lost and Found in the City

BY **CAM HIGGINS** • ILLUSTRATED BY **ALLISON STEINFELD**

LITTLE SIMON
New York   Amsterdam/Antwerp   London   Toronto   Sydney   New Delhi

This book is a work of fiction. Any references to historical events, real people, or real places are used fictitiously. Other names, characters, places, and events are products of the author's imagination, and any resemblance to actual events or places or persons, living or dead, is entirely coincidental.

LITTLE SIMON
An imprint of Simon & Schuster Children's Publishing Division
1230 Avenue of the Americas, New York, New York 10020
First Little Simon hardcover edition February 2025
Copyright © 2025 by Simon & Schuster, LLC
Also available in a Little Simon paperback edition.
All rights reserved, including the right of reproduction in whole or in part in any form.
LITTLE SIMON is a registered trademark of Simon & Schuster, LLC, and associated colophon is a trademark of Simon & Schuster, LLC.
RATNIP is a trademark of Simon & Schuster, LLC.
For information about special discounts for bulk purchases, please contact Simon & Schuster Special Sales at 1-866-506-1949 or business@simonandschuster.com.
The Simon & Schuster Speakers Bureau can bring authors to your live event. For more information or to book an event contact the Simon & Schuster Speakers Bureau at 1-866-248-3049 or visit our website at www.simonspeakers.com.
Designed by Brittany Fetcho
Manufactured in the United States of America 1224 LAK
2 4 6 8 10 9 7 5 3 1
Library of Congress Cataloging-in-Publication Data
Names: Higgins, Cam, author. | Steinfeld, Allison, illustrator.
Title: Lost and found in the city / by Cam Higgins ; illustrated by Allison Steinfeld.
Description: First Little Simon paperback edition. | New York : Little Simon, 2025.
Series: Ratnip ; book 1 | Audience: Ages 5–9. | Summary: Ratnip, a pizza parlor rat and collector of shiny objects, traverses the city to return a lost cellphone to its rightful owner.
Identifiers: LCCN 2024007797 (print) | LCCN 2024007798 (ebook) | ISBN 9781665963459 (paperback) | ISBN 9781665963466 (hardcover) | ISBN 9781665963473 (ebook)
Subjects: CYAC: Rats—Fiction. | Siblings—Fiction. | Lost and found possessions—Fiction Collectors and collecting—Fiction. | LCGFT: Animal fiction.
Classification: LCC PZ7.1.H54497 Lo 2025 (print)
LCC PZ7.1.H54497 (ebook) | DDC [Fic] —dc23
LC record available at https://lccn.loc.gov/2024007797
LC ebook record available at https://lccn.loc.gov/2024007798

Contents

CHAPTER 1: Something Rotten — 1

CHAPTER 2: One of Those Humans — 15

CHAPTER 3: My Favorite Things — 25

CHAPTER 4: At the Bo-Day-Ga — 37

CHAPTER 5: The Pigeons — 49

CHAPTER 6: Which Path to Choose? — 61

CHAPTER 7: Ghosts Aren't Real — 77

CHAPTER 8: Okay, Ghosts Might Be Real — 89

CHAPTER 9: A Helping Paw — 99

CHAPTER 10: Operation Complete — 109

CHAPTER 1
SOMETHING ROTTEN

"First one out of bed is a rotten egg!"

Mmm, rotten egg. I licked my lips. Rotten eggs are the slimiest. And the yummiest!

My nose wiggled as I imagined the deliciously stinky stench of a rotten egg. My whiskers twitched as I almost tasted its gooey greenness.

But then I was jolted awake by the sound of paws racing all around me.

"I win!" my older sister shouted as she leaped out of bed. Her name is Marg. (That's short for Margherita.)

"Aww, *I* wanted to be the rotten egg," whined my other sister, Anchovy.

My brothers, Pepperoni and Veggie, both stepped on me as they woke up and scampered out of the room.

You might have guessed by our names, paws, and whiskery noses that we are pizza rats. Why were we named after pizza toppings? Because we live in an old pizza parlor.

More on that later. First, you need to meet me! My full name is Extra Cheese Scratchy Paws Sniffs-a-Lot. But everyone just calls me—

"Ratnip! You'll be late for breakfast!"

"Coming, Cookie!" I said as I dragged myself out of bed . . . which is an old sock.

I love old socks. They are stinky and cozy. They have a hole at the top for your head and a smaller hole at the bottom where your tail pokes out. Ah, perfect!

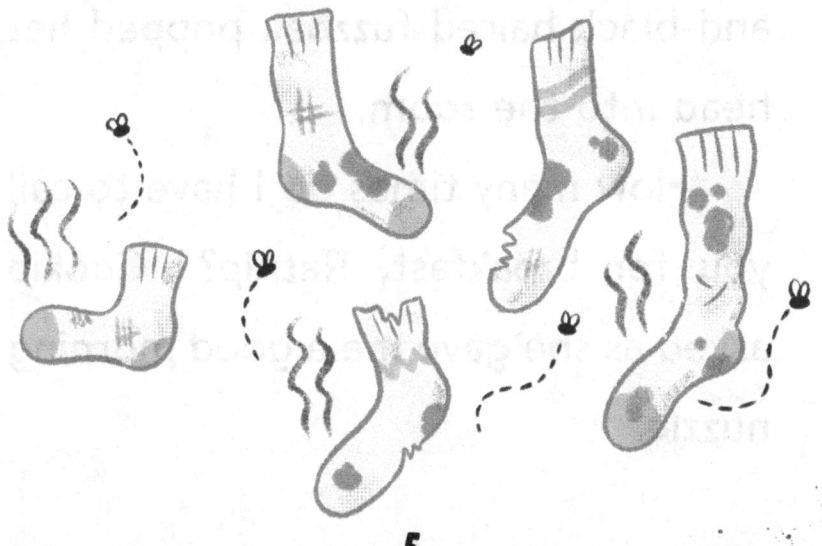

As I stepped onto the perfectly dirty floor of our bedroom, a gray-and-black-haired fuzzball popped her head into the room.

"How many times do I have to call you for breakfast, Ratnip?" Cookie asked as she gave me a good morning nuzzle.

You might be thinking, *Cookie doesn't look like a rat.*

That's because she's not.

Cookie is a raccoon who has lived in the pizza parlor since way before my siblings and I showed up. Ever since we got here, she has taken really good care of us.

"Come on," she said. "Let's go while the sun's still down."

I followed Cookie outside onto the busy sidewalk.

We live in The City, where there are bright lights and loud noises everywhere.

I love it here. There is always something new to explore, different critters to meet, and PLENTY of garbage cans filled with good food!

The closest trash can was on the corner by the pizza parlor. My siblings were already there, digging around for breakfast.

But Cookie and I walked to the small playground at the other end of our street. It is always empty at night, which is when I'm awake.

Even though the playground was farther away, the food was so much better. I'm talking peanut butter sandwich crusts, chocolate chip cookie crumbs, and juice boxes with half the juice still left inside!

My siblings never understood why any critter would walk so far to eat, but Cookie knew what was up.

"Ratnip, you've got some raccoon-level smarts," she said as she pulled out half a pizza slice and tossed it to me.

I knew she was just joking about me having raccoon smarts, but it still made me feel warm and fuzzy inside.

And the pizza was still warm too. Yum!

CHAPTER 2

ONE OF THOSE HUMANS

The pizza was tasty, but now I needed dessert.

I dug deeper in the garbage. Sometimes sweet treats like candy can fall all the way to the bottom.

Then I saw something shiny.

"SCORE!" I yelled. "It's a One-Bite Delight wrapper!"

I held up the gleaming piece of paper like a prize. It sparkled under the streetlights.

"Don't you already have a hundred of those?" Cookie said.

"I wish," I replied. "But this is only my tenth. It's extra shiny, though!"

Cookie took a big gulp from a juice box. "You are one very odd rat. You like wrappers without the food. You collect shiny coins and plastic buttons. If I didn't know better, I'd say you were trying to be like one of those . . . humans."

"Cookie!" I gasped. "You just said the H word!"

RAT FACT: If you just say the word "human," a human will show up. It's true! The City has humans everywhere! Sometimes it feels like there are almost as many humans as rats.

Have you seen a human before? They have big feet that could step on our tails! There are all kinds of them too. Humans with loud, clackity feet. Humans with feet that light up. Humans on wheels. And humans with the weirdest-looking paws.

Most humans come out during the day, while we rats are asleep. But there are always a few that stay out at night too. Like the one that was now coming our way!

Cookie and I dove into the trash can and watched.

ANOTHER RAT FACT: Humans are strange.

This human wore some kind of crown on its head and had whiskers growing from its ears. It began jumping up and down, waving its arms, and running around the playground in circles.

"What is that human doing?" I asked.

"Maybe it has fleas?" said Cookie. "That's what I do when I have fleas. They're so itchy."

"Should we help?" I asked.

"Nah," said Cookie. "It's best to stay away. Humans live in their part of the world, and we live in ours."

We watched as the running human finally left the park. Then we went back to eating.

"Besides," said Cookie after she took a big bite of an apple core, "we don't want to catch fleas from a human. Yuck!"

CHAPTER 3
MY FAVORITE THINGS

When we got home, I ran to the very back of the parlor, where a big, human-size broom leaned against the wall.

I scurried up the broom handle, just like I do every night. I leaped off, sailing through the air, before landing inside . . . my treasure room!

Cookie once said that back when our home was a pizza parlor, this round room was called the "pizza oven." The humans used it to bake their pizzas.

But now I have the space all to myself, and I use it to display my treasures. The curved walls of my room are decorated with a wallpaper collage of my wrappers and paper scraps. And now I had a new one to add to it!

I found my juiciest wad of A-B-C gum. (That stands for "already been chewed.") I bit off a little piece for hanging up my newest One-Bite Delight wrapper. Standing on my hind legs to reach up high, I pressed down with my front paws.

There. I stood back to admire my work.

I've been treasure hunting for as long as I can remember. I like to pick up anything that looks interesting, even if I don't know exactly what it is.

Searching for new treasures is most of the fun, but I take care of my treasures at home too. Especially because everything I collect belongs to me, and not to anyone else. When you have a lot of siblings, that doesn't happen often.

Speaking of siblings . . . just then, Veggie leaped into the room. "It's so hard to get up here," he complained.

"That's the whole point," I said. "The journey is part of the experience!"

"Enough about that," Veggie said. "I found some Bubble Pop! You wanna play?"

"When do I NOT want to play?" I replied, giving him a high five.

Cookie thought Bubble Pop was way too noisy, so we went outside to play. I brought out a coin from my collection too.

The rule was, as long as the coin kept spinning, Veggie and I could jump around and pop the bubbles.

Whoever popped more bubbles won!

Marg was the best at spinning coins, so she spun for us.

"Ready, set, GO!" she yelled.

Pop-pop-pop-pop-pop-pop! Veggie and I jumped on our bubble mats like there was no tomorrow!

"STOP!" Marg shouted. Veggie and I stood in place on our mats, trying to catch our breath. Meanwhile, our siblings counted each of our popped bubbles.

"Fourteen to eight. Veggie wins by six bubbles!" Pepperoni said.

I wanted a rematch, but Veggie shook his head. "Winner's the winner!" he said, grinning. "Besides, we don't have any more bubbles to pop."

"If I go find some, THEN will you give me a rematch before bed?" I asked.

"Okay, fine," Veggie agreed. "But don't expect me to go easy on you!"

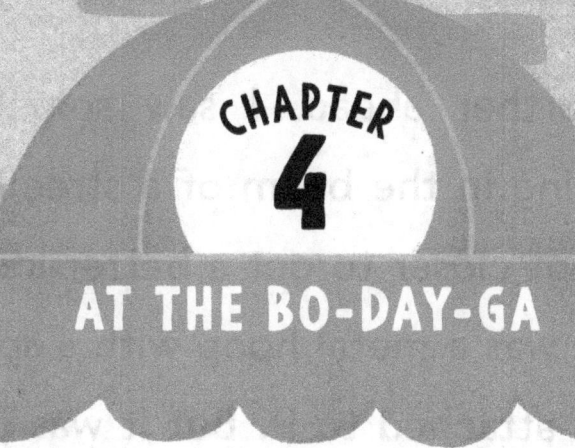

CHAPTER 4
AT THE BO-DAY-GA

I made my way down the street, poking my snout into every nook and cranny.

Near a crack in the sidewalk, I spotted one . . . no, two coins.

"Neat!" I said. It was no Bubble Pop, but I picked them up anyway. I was always looking for more coins.

Farther ahead, I saw something glinting in the beam of a streetlight. I crept closer to get a better look.

It was a metal hoop with a sparkly rock attached to it. But it was just a boring, clear rock. So I pushed it to the side and kept going.

"Hiya, Ratnip!" a small voice said. I looked down to see Rochelle waving her antennae at me.

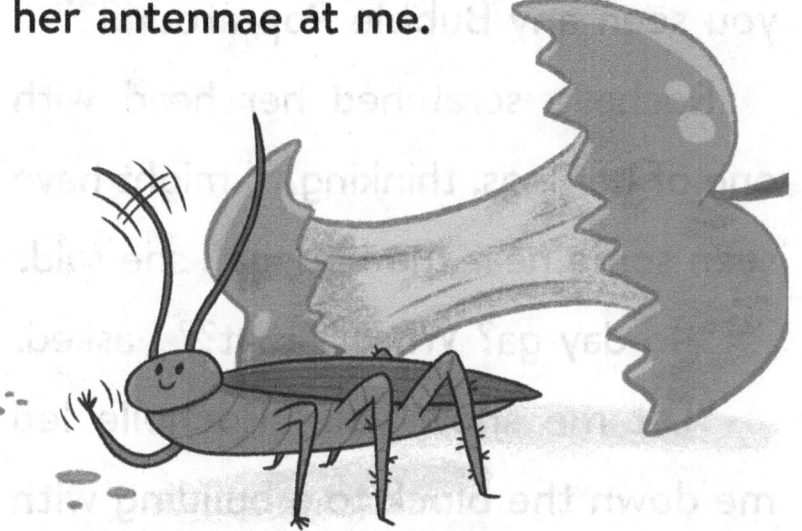

Rochelle is my buddy, and one of the friendliest cockroaches in this neighborhood.

"Doing your daily rounds?" she asked.

"Actually, I'm looking for something specific," I replied. "Have you seen any Bubble Pop around?"

Rochelle scratched her head with one of her legs, thinking. "I might have seen some near the bodega," she said.

"Bo-day-ga? What is that?" I asked.

"Let me show you." Rochelle led me down the block to a building with all its lights on.

"Oh, I know this place!" I said.

Like I mentioned, most humans sleep at night, so their buildings are dark and quiet.

But the bodega is different. It's always open. The rare humans that stay awake at night are always walking out with bags of food.

Outside the bodega, some cardboard boxes rested on the curb. I dove into one of them . . . and found myself in a sea of Bubble Pop!

"I hit the JACKPOT!" I squeaked, stuffing as much Bubble Pop as I could fit into my bag. "Thanks, Rochelle!"

When my bag was close to bursting, I jumped out onto the sidewalk again. And that's when I saw it.

The Brand New, Totally Interesting, Super Special Thing I'd Never Seen Before.

It was a black rectangle, and almost as long as I was. I reached out with a paw, and The Thing felt smooth and cold.

Next, I sniffed. It smelled like human. But then again, almost everything in The City smells like human.

My heart started beating faster, but in a good way. It wasn't every day that I found something totally new on the streets!

"What is it?" Rochelle asked.

"I don't know," I replied. "But . . . I KNOW I want to take it home!"

There was only one question: How?

CHAPTER 5
THE PIGEONS

I grabbed on to The Thing with my front paws and started dragging it along the sidewalk.

But I wasn't so good at balancing on my hind legs. Plus, The Thing's body was so slippery that it kept falling through my paws.

Time for another idea.

I began nudging The Thing along the sidewalk with my snout. That quickly grew tiring, though.

As I was rubbing my sore nose, someone called out, "Hi, Ratnip. Hi, Rochelle."

First, I looked left. Nothing. Then I looked right, but no one was there, either.

Then I looked up. Two pigeons came flying down from the sky.

It was Jinny and Ian!

"What do you have there?" Ian asked.

"I'm not sure what it is," I said, "but I'm going to add it to my collection."

The two pigeons looked at each other. "Would you take a mysterious Thing home?" Jinny asked Ian.

"I would not," Ian answered.

They flapped their wings and pecked at The Thing, when it suddenly started flopping around and buzzing!

Jinny and Ian took off in fright. When they were safely perched on a fence, they shouted, "That Thing is ALIVE!"

I gently sniffed it again. "It doesn't smell like it's alive."

When it stopped flopping around, I picked up The Thing with my teeth and continued dragging it along the sidewalk. That's when The Thing buzzed again!

It lit up as bright as any streetlight and displayed a picture of a human.

The very one I'd seen in the playground during breakfast!

"Oh NO!" I gasped. "I was about to break one of the most important rules of treasure hunting!"

"What's the rule?" Rochelle asked.

"Never take something that belongs to someone else," I said. "Because that's not collecting. That's stealing."

Jinny and Ian fluttered back down to look at the picture.

"So, this human owns this Thing?" Jinny said. "We should all fly away before it comes looking for it."

I puffed out my cheeks. "Well, some of us don't have wings. Plus, treasure hunters don't just leave treasures on the street! I need to bring this Thing back to its true owner."

Rochelle peered at the picture. "I know this human," she said. "It lives in the brick building over there."

She pointed her antenna down the street.

"Can you show me the way?" I asked Rochelle. Then I turned to Jinny and Ian. "Do you want to join us?"

"Oh, no, no, no." Ian ruffled his feathers. "No way."

"We couldn't," Jinny added quickly.

I sighed. That was the thing about pigeons. They could be so . . . flighty.

But at least Rochelle was willing to help me with . . .

CHAPTER 6
WHICH PATH TO CHOOSE?

A jingling sound startled us. It was a human and a dog walking by.

The dog spotted Jinny and Ian.

"Pigeon! Pigeon!" the dog barked out, paying no attention to Rochelle or me.

Jinny and Ian puffed out their chests, trying to look brave.

The dog dropped to his belly, then sprang up to run toward them.

But the human was holding on to a rope tied around the dog. It stopped the dog from getting too close to Jinny and Ian.

Wait a minute! That gave me an idea. I could find something to tie The Thing to me too. That would surely make it easier to carry.

Jinny and Ian cooed angrily as the dog and the human walked away.

I turned to the pigeons. "I just thought of a great idea! Could you help me find a cord or a rope?"

"Maybe we could do that," Jinny replied.

"But we can't promise," Ian added.

That was about as close to a "yes" as I was ever going to get from a pigeon.

Jinny and Ian took off into the night. Meanwhile, I sniffed around for some gum. Luckily, that was always easy to find in The City. I found a big pink wad of A-B-C gum on the edge of the sidewalk.

"Watch this," I said to Rochelle. I scraped off a couple of pieces. Then I pulled out the coins I'd picked up earlier. I used the gum to stick the coins to the sides of The Thing, sort of like a pair of wheels.

"Smart thinking, Ratnip!" Rochelle said, clapping her legs together.

After a few minutes, Jinny and Ian returned with a long wire. It looked like it would be fun to chew . . . but that would have to wait until after our mission was completed.

I tied the wire around The Thing, then looped the other end around my waist.

I took a few steps forward. The Thing rolled behind me. It was rickety, but it worked!

"There are two ways to reach the human's brick building," Rochelle explained. "We could keep going down this street."

I stared down the block. It stretched out forever in front of us.

"Or we turn left and take a shortcut through a little park," Rochelle said.

"The *HAUNTED* park?" Ian said, his feathers quivering.

"What do you mean?" I asked.

"Well, I don't know if I believe it," Rochelle said. "But some say there are ghosts living in the park."

"Sad ghosts," Jinny added. "Once, our robin friends said the whole park burst into tears. It just started to CRY! Can you imagine how sad those ghosts must be to make a whole park cry?"

I don't mind getting wet. After all, we rats are pretty good swimmers. But I don't know if I'm good enough to swim through GHOST tears.

I do not like ghosts.

I looked at the long street in front of me. Then I glanced toward the haunted park.

Then The Thing lit up again. *Buzz, buzz!* it said, before going dark and quiet. It was almost like it was telling me to take the shortcut.

The two pigeons shook their heads. "You are one brave rat," Jinny said, before she and Ian flew away. "Good luck with the ghosts!"

CHAPTER 7

GHOSTS AREN'T REAL

Rochelle and I entered the park.

Unlike most places in The City, this park had bushes and flowers. The ground felt soft and squishy under my paws. It was amazing!

But there was no time to stop and smell the roses. Not when there were ghosts around.

I moved as quickly as I could, keeping close to Rochelle. The only sound was The Thing bumping along the ground behind us.

Suddenly, one of the bushes next to me started trembling.

"The ghosts!" Rochelle whispered, clutching my front leg. "They're real!"

We started backing away, but my paw caught on the wire connecting me to The Thing. I tripped and fell backward. Rochelle, who was still holding on to my leg, fell with me.

But it wasn't a ghost that tumbled out of the bushes. Nope. It was a squirrel.

"Ah ha ha! Gotcha!" He squealed with laughter. "Oh, squirrel-friends, you should have seen the looks on your faces!"

His fuzzy tail bounced up and down as he rolled around on the ground, laughing and laughing.

Rat Fact: Squirrels are silly critters. And they don't normally come out at night.

But I know this squirrel. His name is Ernie, and he is famous for two things.

First, he never, ever sleeps. Second, he is kind of . . . uh . . . nutty.

I mean, I guess that's what happens when you don't sleep.

"That was HA-HA-hilarious," Ernie said, pushing himself up. "You both looked scared out of your minds!"

"Okay, Ernie, you got us," I said.

But Rochelle was so upset, she started hissing. "That was MEAN!" she yelled, then scurried off.

"Wait!" I called, but cockroaches are fast. Rochelle disappeared before I could even chase after her.

"Aw, come on," Ernie said. "It was just a joke."

Now it was my turn to be upset. Without Rochelle to help, I was never going to return The Thing!

"Ernie! We were on a VERY important mission," I said. "We need to find this human."

I pressed The Thing with my paws, and the human's face appeared again.

Ernie looked at the picture. "Sorry, pal," he answered. "Humans all look the same to me."

I rolled my eyes. Ernie may be the least helpful squirrel in the history of squirrels.

"Well, thanks for nothing, then," I said.

But Ernie blocked my path and flicked his fluffy tail.

"Did you really believe ghosts live here?" he asked. "I mean, everyone knows ghosts . . . aren't . . . real."

Ernie's eyes were glued to something behind me. His tail slowly stopped twitching, and his mouth dropped wide open.

"Ha-ha, very funny," I told him. "You can't fool me twice."

But then Ernie's eyes got even wider, and my paws started getting sweaty.

Was Ernie really seeing a ghost behind me?

CHAPTER 8
OKAY, GHOSTS MIGHT BE REAL

I turned and stared into the darkness.

Something moved in the shadows. Something big.

"IT'S A GHOST!" Ernie hollered. He bolted away faster than if a dog were chasing him.

I tried to run too. But The Thing was so heavy, it held me back.

The ghost shadow inched closer and closer. Soon a dark shape floated right in front of me.

  I was all alone . . . trapped . . . and about to be eaten by a ghost!
  Okay, maybe ghosts don't eat rats, but how could I be sure?

"Stop, ghost!" I yelled. "My name is Ratnip. I am taking a shortcut through your park. Do NOT eat me, or I will give you a very bad ghost tummy ache!"

The ghost shape stepped forward.

"What if I'm a cat instead of a ghost?" a black alley cat asked, towering in front of me.

Most rats would be really scared now, because alley cats have sharp claws and sharp teeth. And they're always hungry.

But I am not like most rats. In fact, cats LIKE me.

Cookie says I'm so sweet, not even a cat would ever harm a whisker on my head. And that's why everyone calls me . . .

"Ratnip? Yoo-hoo?" the cat said.

"Katy!" I said, breathing a sigh of relief. "I'm so glad you're not a ghost!"

"Why are you dragging a phone behind you?" she said, pointing to The Thing.

"Phone?" I repeated. "Well, call this Thing what you want, but I need to get it back to the human who lost it."

Katy swatted The Thing, and it lit up again. "Oh, THIS human. It's always running around in circles!"

"Yeah, that's the one," I said. "Wait! Do you know where this human lives?"

Katy pointed her tail to the left. "Over there, I think," she said.

Woohoo! The mission was back on track. Time for a happy dance! Except I was still tangled up in the wire so instead of dancing, I went . . . *fwomp*.

"Ah, little friend," said Katy as she untangled my paws. "What would you do without me?"

I leaned back and watched the night sky get brighter and brighter. Dawn was near, which meant I needed to be home soon or else Cookie would come looking for me.

This treasure rescuer was running out of time.

CHAPTER 9
A HELPING PAW

Katy must have seen the worried look on my rat face. "Hey, Ratnip," she said. "I can help you carry The Thing."

I gasped. "Really?"

Katy shrugged. "Wouldn't YOU help someone if you could?"

She was right. After all, I was trying to help The Thing find its human.

"All right, off we go!" said Katy. She turned around, but then she just kept standing in place. I didn't know what she was up to, so I stood there beside her.

After a few seconds, she blinked her yellow eyes at me and said, "Well, aren't you going to climb on?"

I gasped. I had never heard of another critter riding on the back of an alley cat.

"Katy, it would be an honor!" I squealed.

I shimmied up onto her back and nestled into her fur with The Thing cradled between my paws.

"Hold on tight," Katy said. Then we were off!

RAT **F**ACT: Alley cats move FAST. Cat legs are like a hundred times longer than rat legs, so I guess it makes sense. But she was so speedy, I felt the air ruffling my fur!

We must have been quite a sight. Everyone we passed stopped to stare at us.

Ernie gawked from a tree branch. "Am I dreaming?" he said.

Jinny and Ian were perched on top of a stop sign. "*Coooool!*"

Even Rochelle popped her head out from under a sewer cover as we bolted past.

"A rat riding on a cat? Now I've seen everything!" she said.

All along, I held on to The Thing as tightly as I could. I was a knight on a very important errand!

Finally, Katy came to a stop in front of a big brick building.

I looked across the street and saw another brick building. In fact, all the buildings looked the same to me.

"Um, are you sure this is the right one?" I asked.

"The funny running human?" Katy said. "I'm one hundred percent certain. Now hop down, little buddy."

I thanked Katy over and over, but she just licked her paw and took off without saying goodbye.

Cats can be like that sometimes.

CHAPTER 10
OPERATION COMPLETE

Leaving things for humans to find is not easy. I needed the perfect spot for The Thing or else it might be lost forever.

If I left it on the stairs, humans would crush it with their enormous feet. But if I left it hidden, the human might not notice it at all.

And if I tried to leave The Thing inside its home . . . well, humans do not like rats in their homes.

But every home has a front door, so that's where I headed.

I scampered up the steps and untied the wire from around my waist. Well, I TRIED to untie it. Oh, why are wires so easy to tangle yet so hard to untangle?

RATNIP FACT: Sometimes I forget I'm a rat.

Like when I am trying to untie wires with my rat paws . . . and I could have been using my teeth. Chewing through it is the easiest—and tastiest—way to untie anything!

Suddenly the ground around me started to rumble. Then I heard a muffled stomping, growing louder and louder. All rats know that sound: human footsteps!

Time to dine and dash! I chomped through the last piece of wire connecting me to The Thing and scrambled away just as the door swung open.

Clink! The door hit The Thing. I winced, hoping it wasn't damaged.

A human bent down. And it wasn't just any human. It was THE human!

My heart was beating fast . . . and rat hearts already beat ten times faster than human hearts!

The human looked at The Thing. "What in the world?" it said.

"Pick it up! Pick it up!" I whispered. Oh, humans can move so slow sometimes!

The human untied the wire and pulled off the coins and gum. It made a face, like it was really confused and grossed out.

But then the human tapped on The Thing and peered into its screen. Its face turned from confusion to joy. Letting out a shriek of delight, it jumped around and hugged The Thing close.

Phew! Operation Return The Thing to the Human was complete!

I looked up at the sky. It was much lighter now, but I knew how to get home before sunrise. I just had to run.

All the way home, I was filled with a warm, fuzzy feeling about my lucky night. I found lost treasure, helped a human, and even rode on an alley cat's back.

Of course, I ran out of time for my Bubble Pop rematch. But hey, that's what tomorrow is for!

There is only one sure thing about being a rat in The City: You never know what adventures you'll find!

Here's a peek at Ratnip's next adventure!

Have you ever wanted to eat something so badly, you couldn't think about anything else?

Now you might be wondering: Don't rats feel that way about every kind of food?

And you would be correct. I like

to eat pretty much everything.

But it doesn't mean I like all food the same amount.

Imagine there's a great big chocolate cake sitting on a table. It has swirly frosting on the outside, moist yellow cake on the inside, and it's covered all over in sparkly sprinkles.

Then imagine this: under the table, there's a slice of old pizza. It's fallen cheese side down. The pepperoni is cold. Who knows how long it's been there, but it's starting to stink.

Both foods would be tasty. But only one of them would make my fur stand on end and my whiskers go *zing* with attention.

I mean, who would EVER choose cake over stinky pizza?

Mmm. PIZZA. It's my favorite food. In fact, it was exactly what I wanted right now.

I gazed up at the old pizza menus hanging inside my house. Way back when, this building used to be a pizza parlor. If only it could cook up some fresh pies for me now!